TABLE OF CONTENTS

© 2015 Emek Hebrew Academy
Teichman Family Torah Center

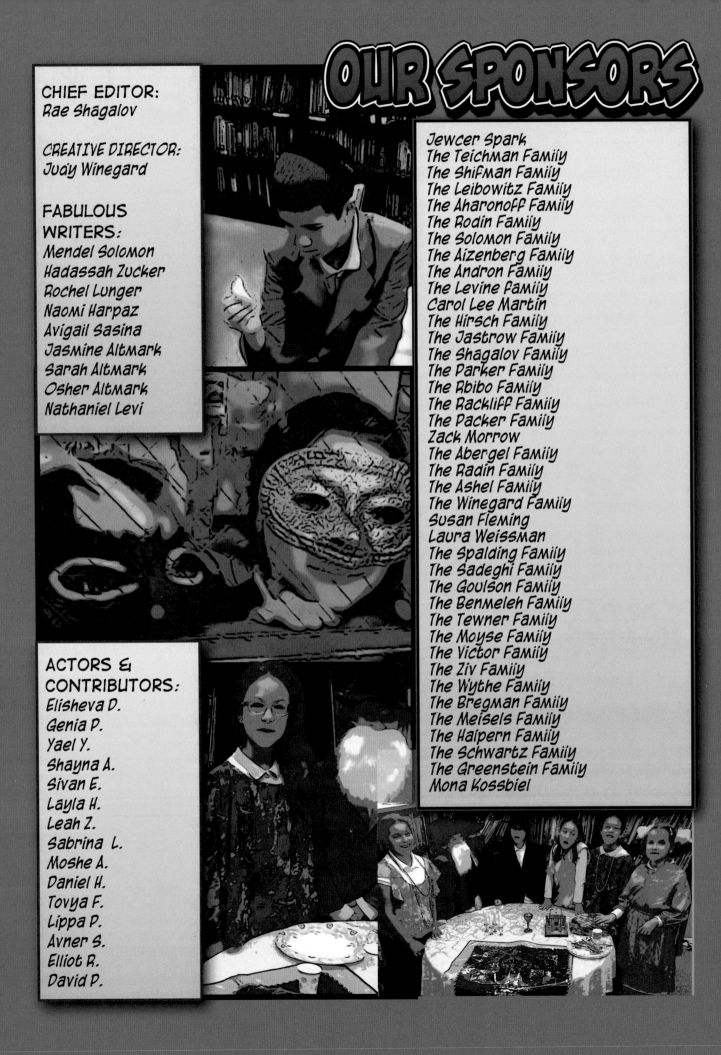

OUR SPONSORS

CHIEF EDITOR:
Rae Shagalov

CREATIVE DIRECTOR:
Judy Winegard

FABULOUS
WRITERS:
Mendel Solomon
Hadassah Zucker
Rochel Lunger
Naomi Harpaz
Avigail Sasina
Jasmine Altmark
Sarah Altmark
Osher Altmark
Nathaniel Levi

ACTORS &
CONTRIBUTORS:
Elisheva D.
Genia P.
Yael Y.
Shayna A.
Sivan E.
Layla H.
Leah Z.
Sabrina L.
Moshe A.
Daniel H.
Tovya F.
Lippa P.
Avner S.
Elliot R.
David P.

Jewcer Spark
The Teichman Family
The Shifman Family
The Leibowitz Family
The Aharonoff Family
The Rodin Family
The Solomon Family
The Aizenberg Family
The Andron Family
The Levine Family
Carol Lee Martin
The Hirsch Family
The Jastrow Family
The Shagalov Family
The Parker Family
The Rbibo Family
The Rackliff Family
The Packer Family
Zack Morrow
The Abergel Family
The Radin Family
The Ashel Family
The Winegard Family
Susan Fleming
Laura Weissman
The Spalding Family
The Sadeghi Family
The Goulson Family
The Benmeleh Family
The Tewner Family
The Moyse Family
The Victor Family
The Ziv Family
The Wythe Family
The Bregman Family
The Meisels Family
The Halpern Family
The Schwartz Family
The Greenstein Family
Mona Kossbiel

SUPER RABBI*!

ONCE THERE WAS A GREAT RABBI.

WHO PRAYED & LEARNED TORAH ALL DAY.

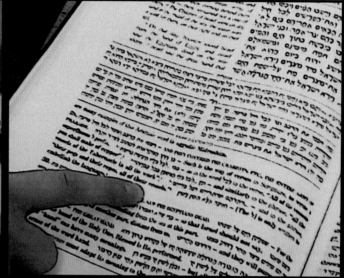

ONE DAY, HE WAS PRAYING WHEN SUDDENLY THE PAGE RIPPED!

HE KISSED THE SIDDUR**...

RRRRIPPP!!

* A RABBI IS A JEWISH TEACHER AND LEADER

** A SIDDUR IS A JEWISH PRAYER BOOK

WHERE AM I?

WHEN HE WOKE UP HE WAS IN A MYSTERIOUS ROOM.

SUDDENLY, A VOICE SAID.......

I AM HASHEM*

DON'T BE SCARED

YOU ARE NOW A NAVI**

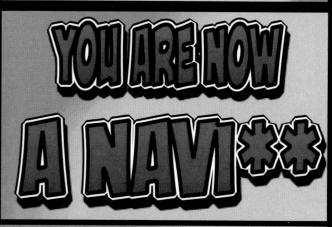

YOU CAN ALSO FLY

YOU ARE NOW

SUPER RABBI!

*HASHEM MEANS, "THE NAME" AND IS WHAT WE CALL G-D TO BE RESPECTFUL.

**A NAVI IS A PROPHET, A HOLY PERSON WHO HAS VISIONS FROM G-D.

BACK AT SUPER RABBI'S TABLE......

I'M GETTING A PROPHECY....

SUPER RABBI SAW THE BAD GUYS ROBBING AN ATM!

THEY'RE TAKING BAGS OF MONEY!!

WE HAVE TO STOP THIS!

SUPER RABBI GOT A VISION AND HASHEM SAID...
LOST AND FOUND
YOUR FRIEND IS IN HERE

DAVID TRAILING NOT SO FAR BEHIND.

HASHEM MADE FOOTPRINTS APPEAR INSIDE SO THEY COULD FOLLOW THE BAD GUYS.

NOW SUPER RABBI GOT HIS FIRST GOOD LOOK AT HIS OPPONENT.

NICE TO MEET YOU SUPER RABBI. I'VE HEARD SO MUCH ABOUT YOU.

21

THE BOSS BLACKED OUT.

WHEN THE BOSS WOKE UP, HE TRIED TO ATTACK!

GRRRR!!

THEY DISARMED HIM AND PUT HIM IN JAIL.

HA! HA! HA!

AND DAVID GOT HIS REVENGE BY LOCKING THE DOOR.

MEANWHILE, THE OTHERS WERE GETTING AWAY !

23

SUPER RABBI FLEW
TO THE RESCUE

24

SUPER RABBI FLEW BACK WITH THEM IN HIS HANDS.

GRRRR!!

HE PUT THEM IN JAIL.

ARGHHH!

25

THE LESSON IS TO ALWAYS...

TRUST HASHEM

THE END!

26

27

THE SHABBAT ANGELS' CONTEST

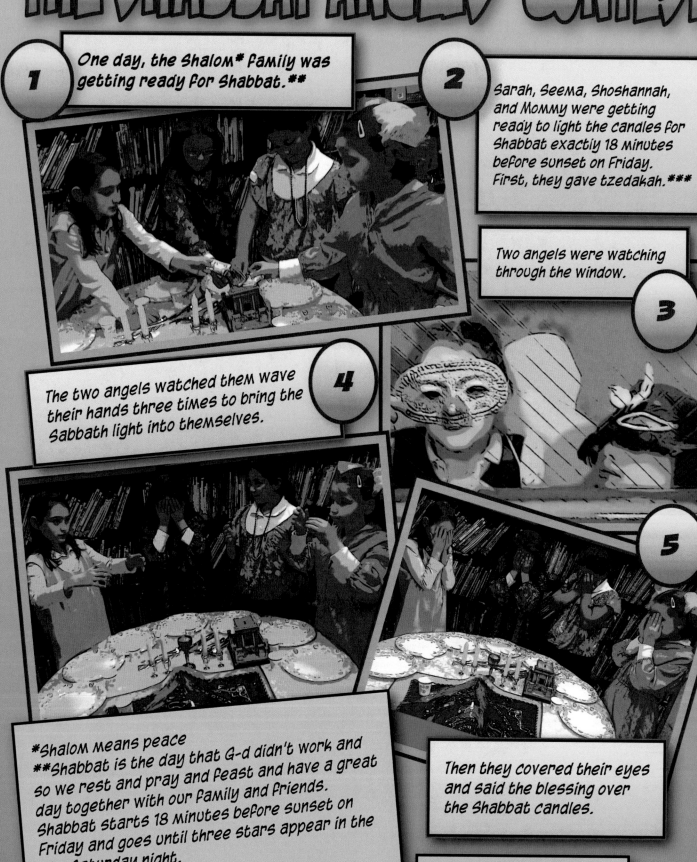

1 One day, the Shalom* family was getting ready for Shabbat.**

2 Sarah, Seema, Shoshannah, and Mommy were getting ready to light the candles for Shabbat exactly 18 minutes before sunset on Friday. First, they gave tzedakah.***

Two angels were watching through the window.

3

4 The two angels watched them wave their hands three times to bring the Sabbath light into themselves.

5

*Shalom means peace
**Shabbat is the day that G-d didn't work and so we rest and pray and feast and have a great day together with our family and friends. Shabbat starts 18 minutes before sunset on Friday and goes until three stars appear in the sky Saturday night.

Then they covered their eyes and said the blessing over the Shabbat candles.

***Tzedakah is charity.

MAY IT BE LIKE THIS NEXT SHABBAT!

6

The Yetzer Tov** angel was very happy.

*AMEN MEANS THAT WE BELIEVE THAT G-D SHOULD MAKE THE BLESSING THAT WAS JUST SAID COME TRUE.

*AMEN.

7

The Yetzer Hara*** angel made a scowly face but she had to say amen.

Abba, Zaidy and Shimmy Shalom came home from shul.****

8

Everyone stood by the Shabbat table. Abba and Zaidy started singing the song Shalom Aleichem. The family was welcoming the Shabbat angels by singing the song.

9

**Yetzer Tov: The good side of you
***Yetzer Hara: The side of you that makes you do stuff that isn't good
****Shul: A synagogue, where Jews pray together

29

Everyone got up and helped Mommy clear the table.
30
Zaidy waved his hand and said...
GOOD-BYE SHABBAT ANGELS! SEE YOU NEXT WEEK!
31
MAY IT BE LIKE THIS NEXT SHABBAT.
MAY IT BE LIKE THIS NEXT SHABBAT.
32
And everyone answered...
AMEN!!!
THE END

ALWAYS ASK BEFORE YOU TAKE SOMETHING THAT DOESN'T BELONG TO YOU.

People need to have friends

YOU KNOW YOU WOULD LIKE TO HAVE A FRIEND. WHEN YOU HELP SOMEONE ELSE HAVE FRIENDS, YOU ARE DOING THE MITZVAH OF LOVING YOUR FRIEND LIKE YOU LOVE YOURSELF.

GLOSSARY
JEWISH WORDS TO KNOW!

Abba: Father

Amen: Means that we believe that G-d should make the blessing that was just said come true

Blessing: Praising, thanking or asking G-d for the things we need

Challah: The delicious braided Sabbath bread. Before eating bread, we wash our hands three times on each hand with a special two-handled washing cup

Hashem: The name of G-d is so holy that we don't want to say it out of reverence. Instead we say Hashem, which means, "The Name." That's also why we put a dash in the word G-d when we write it.

Kiddush: The start of the Shabbat meal begins with the blessing over the wine or grape juice.

Mitzvah: A commandment from G-d in the Torah that we should follow to connect to G-d

Navi: A prophet, a holy person who has visions from G-d

Rabbi: A teacher and leader who is learned in Torah

Shabbat: Shabbat (also called Shabbos or the Sabbath) is the day that G-d didn't work and so we rest, pray and feast and have a great day together with our family and friends. Shabbat starts 18 minutes before sunset on Friday and goes until three stars appear in the sky Saturday night.

Shalom: Peace

Shalom Aleichem: Means "Peace Be With Us," and is the first song we sing at the Shabbat table on Friday nights

Shul: A synagogue where Jews go to pray

Siddur: Prayerbook

Torah: The five Books of Moses; the Holy Bible

Tzedakah: Charity money

Yetzer Hara: The side of you that makes you do stuff that isn't good

Yetzer Tov: The good side of you

Zaidy: Grandfather

Zemirot: Traditional Shabbat songs

ABOUT US

Why We Created This Comic

We looked on Amazon.com, the largest online bookseller in the world, and saw that there were hardly any Jewish comics for kids, so we decided to create one. We are students at a Jewish school but we know that not every Jewish kid is lucky enough to get to learn about Torah and mitzvahs. We wanted to create a comic that ALL Jewish Children would enjoy, even if they didn't know much about being Jewish.

How We Created This Comic

This comic was really fun to make. First, we created a storyboard for each story in the comic. Then we made props and dressed up in costumes to act out the story. We used the Toon Camera app to shoot the pictures so that we would look like comic book characters. We used the Comic Life app to design the pages and add the narration boxes and speech bubbles. We had to think about what was important about being Jewish. Then we had to make sure that our Jewish idea came across in our story in a fun way. We think Project-Based-Learning is the best kind of 21st century education!

DO YOU LIKE OUR COMIC?
PLEASE LEAVE A REVIEW FOR US ON AMAZON!

Inspiring Minds, Joining Hearts.

emek

EMEK HEBREW ACADEMY
TEICHMAN FAMILY TORAH CENTER

Made in the USA
Columbia, SC
17 June 2022

61863386R00024